CARLOS

CASARES

His Excellency

CARLOS
CASARES

His Excellency

Translated from Galician
by Jacob Rogers

XUNTA DE GALICIA   Small Stations Press

Small Stations Press
Registered address: 20 Dimitar Manov Street, 1408 Sofia, Bulgaria
You can order books and contact the publisher at
www.smallstations.com

First published in Galician as *Ilustrísima* by Editorial Galaxia S.A., Vigo, in 1980. All scriptural quotations are taken from the 1899 American edition of the Douay-Rheims Bible.

The publishers gratefully acknowledge the use of the cover image of Carlos Casares supplied by the Carlos Casares Foundation in Vigo, and the help received from its secretary, Gustavo Adolfo Garrido.

ISBN 978-954-384-067-0
Legal deposit C 149-2017

*To my uncle Xosé Mouriño, abbot of Beiro,
good representative of a long family tradition of priests,
canons, and bishops, this novel that in a certain way
I owed him.*

*Be gone fiend, you have no power
over my heart.*

Paul Valéry

I

His Excellency's unlimited patience was starting to overflow the generous limits of his round anatomy. At the end of the report he'd just finished reading, troubling and severe, there had also been news added for him in pencil that did nothing but increase the dull irritation he'd started to feel towards his attendant a couple of months ago. For that reason he wanted to eat alone. He gobbled up the consommé, delicately complained because the steak was overdone, asked for a couple slices of ham in exchange, made a mixture of apples and cheese as a kind of dessert, and gave orders that the coffee be served to him in the Saint Ignatius Lounge.

It was his favorite nook on summer days, especially for taking a catnap after lunch and before the study period, which began at exactly four o'clock each afternoon. The thick, red velvet curtains prevented needing to half-close the shutters to fend off the sun, and the large armchairs, the most comfortable in the whole house, invited sleep right there, without having to go through the (for him) insurmountable discomfort of getting into bed at those hours. Only the swarms of flies that would gather in that area, possibly attracted by the nearby presence of the horses, which had their stables right below, stopped that pleasant lounge from being exactly what His Excellency desired.

He was already impatient for them to arrive with the coffee. The servant's exit and the soft thud of the heavy chestnut door closing behind him were the cue to get comfortable. He unbuttoned his cassock, untied his shoelaces, and covered his bald patch with a white cloth to fend off the flies. Then he rested his head on his right hand, stretched out his legs as far as he could, and let himself be lulled by the familiar noises rising up from the street. He remained like that, peacefully sleepy, for more than an hour.

But that afternoon he wasn't able to catch a wink. The memory of Don Xenaro's report grated inside his head like a babble of infuriated words. Ever since the Italian Pietro Barbagelatta had the idea of setting up a cinematograph in the city, His Excellency hadn't had any peace. First there was the paperwork with the town hall to deny him a permit, which resulted in the disaster he'd predicted beforehand. Then came the pressure on the owner of the building to not rent it out, which turned out to be equally fruitless. Now that thoughtless and anti-evangelical implication, which he swore to himself he wouldn't allow no matter what.

He still hadn't had time to think of a radical solution when the soft and childlike voice of Don Xenaro saying, "Your Excellency, Your Excellency," from the other side of the door disrupted his peace once again. He let a good bit of time pass by without saying a word, and when he'd already decided not to answer, he changed his mind because he figured the attendant would end up coming into the room without his permission. He wasn't wrong. Before authorizing him to come in, the vast and solid butterball appeared in the doorway, asking loudly if His Excellency was feeling well.

"I feel perfectly fine."

"Would Your Excellency like me to order him a chamomile tea?" persisted the attendant.

"No, no. Thank you though," said the bishop, pointing at a seat so Don Xenaro would sit down.

Then he buttoned his cassock and began to tie his shoelaces. He did it calmly, aware of how the forced position gave him an advantage over his adversary and allowed him to adjust the colors in his face, still intensely red. When he sat up, he realized he was wearing the fly-swatting cloth on his head and felt ridiculous. However he decided not to take it off. In that way he regained power over the situation, as was demonstrated in Don Xenaro's nervousness and his fidgety hands, and he could successfully face the dreaded proposal he imagined was going to be presented to him through his attendant's mouth.

But he was wrong. The latter's nervousness was not that of someone who comes to command something, but that of someone who's going to request. It was a favor. His nephew Antonio Biempica, the firstborn son of his sister Teresa, in whose home His Excellency had tasted the best stew of his life, had eaten the tastiest lamb that had ever caressed his choosy palate, and had polished off a flan that had neither comparison nor equal in the whole diocese, wanted to enter the seminary and be fast-tracked to the priesthood. His age suggested that shortcut to him. And his wisdom, the bishop suspected, wouldn't take him much further.

His Excellency laughed gleefully to himself, although outwardly he tried as best he could to form a serious bishop-like expression, took the cloth off his head, smiled softly to align the outside of his face with the internal enjoyment he felt, and before giving an answer held off by asking, with a kind of intentional unhurriedness:

"Do you know the story of Don Braulio Fuentes, a priest from my native diocese who I had dealings with at the Mondoñedo seminary?"

His Excellency already knew the response would be a negative before formulating the question, but he waited until Don Xenaro said that he didn't. Then he lingered with his happy and green eyes fixed upon him for a while, and afterwards spoke to him about that fast-track priest, as dopey as he was saintly, the anecdotes about whom made two generations of Mondoñedo priests cackle with laughter.

The story goes that this Don Braulio, on the day of his first mass, come the solemn hour of consecration he leaned over the altar as the ritual prescribed and stayed like that for five long minutes, before the surprise and anxiousness of the sponsoring priest, who couldn't understand such a delay even if allowing him the generous window usually given to a first-time priest so that he can recover from the emotion. Two more minutes having gone by, in an audible whisper, the sponsor begged him: "Consecrate, Braulio!" The other, without even moving, twisting his mouth to one side and gesturing with his heavy head, asked: "Do what?" "The host," responded the assisting priest. "I already ate it!" answered Don Braulio.

Don Xenaro laughed torrentially, with convulsions that went down like ocean waves from his double chin to his chest, where they rested for a few seconds to then die softly in his gut. His Excellency was pleased by his attendant's happiness. He also thought how that kind of laughter, boisterous and cheerful, pushed away from the conversation, at least on this occasion, the topic of the cinematograph. Although the bishop was well aware of the man's weakness and the moral cowardice that had paralyzed him so many times in his presence, he wasn't ignorant of the transformations in character which had taken place in him over the past two years. Pushed by conflicts of conscience and spurred on by a sincere mysticism which he was brought to by his inability to understand the religious crisis threatening the Church, he was able to gather enough strength to form a brave and prophetic expression.

When His Excellency had arrived at the diocese, Don Xenaro was the seminary's majordomo. Over the course of a private audience, he'd asked to be heard in confession by the prelate. The tears shed, the internal struggles and battles, gigantic like his body, touched the bishop's compassion deeply, and he asked him to be his attendant right there. It was a mistake. For years he'd hardly created any problems, but lately he'd become an uncomfortable collaborator. His few gifts of the intellectual kind, and a scrupulous loyalty to a conscience tormented by fear, made him ideal prey for those who worked behind closed doors against His Excellency's diocesan politics.

As he laughed, the bishop contemplated his complete lack of grace. Big and clumsy, his incredibly long and strong arms, his enormous stomach, everything about him had an abnormal and disproportionate dimension to it. His Excellency pictured the pitiful adolescent melancholies, the hurtful deceptions in front of the mirror at the beginning of his youth, his first defeats at social connection. He was going to take pity on him, substituting animosity for mercy, but he didn't have time. Almost in one jump, the attendant stood up, kissed the bishop's ring forcefully, reached the door in a couple of strides and left. Underneath the smile with which he tried to soften the involuntary gruffness of his clumsy ways was concealed a cocky expression that ended up darkening His Excellency's bright eyes.

II

His Excellency was busy contemplating the morning-time happiness of the streets from the landau's little window, indifferent to the sermon Don Xenaro launched into at his side about the dangers that confront souls during the summer. Upon passing by the ravine, from far away he could make out, blurry in the dog-day heat, no less than two dozen boys bathing in the river. He then felt a kind of physical and pagan call which forced him to recite a quick and fervent prayer to himself. This sight only made the visit he was about to begin in that moment even more painful. He didn't like to give mass in the nuns' chapel during the summer months. It was unbearably hot and he was also incapable of getting used to that aroma of lemon verbena which impregnated the whole convent. And as if that weren't enough, Sister Sabina.

He'd been at the point of a ban on her being called a saint in his presence many times, but he didn't dare. And even less since, on his last *ad limina* visit, he'd heard from the lips of a conceited cardinal this same descriptor applied to that nun who the priesthood held up as the pride and joy of the diocese. In all honesty, he couldn't stand her. He remembered her every day at mass, and it was to her he owed the chore of having to do a small and daily act of contrition so he could go to the communion table without a shadow or a show of displeasure towards that Sister in Christ. He constantly promised to try harder on the path to overcoming the hostility he felt towards her, but he'd become convinced it was impossible a long time ago. She was one of his crosses.

His other was right beside him. Don Xenaro was occupied in telling him about the sister's latest miracle. And although he continued to look intently through the little window, offering his back to the attendant, he couldn't avoid hearing the latest news the latter was recounting to him. Luckily for everyone, as if for the honor of the diocese and as an example of Christianity, God spoke every day more clearly through the small and rose-like mouth (that's exactly how he referred to it) of Sister Sabina. The Lord's latest intervention had taken place the afternoon of the day before, during the rosary: Sister Sabina had levitated.

His Excellency recited Jesus's saintly name to himself two times in a row, and it took him a great deal of effort to repress his immediate desire to make the sign of the cross. But he held on, and without changing his attitude, with the same feigned indifference he'd adopted since the beginning, he continued to listen to his interlocutor. He couldn't see the man's face, but he had a clear picture of the white, nearly ill color of his cheeks, the excited shining of his dark eyes, and the dumbfounded bulge of his discolored lips. He talked about the nun as if she were Saint Teresa of Ávila and was even prepared to compare them. Actually that was what he was doing at that moment. His Excellency was bold enough to interrupt him:

"Saint Teresa is on the altars."

Surprised by the unexpected nature of the observation, Don Xenaro managed to respond:

"Sister Sabina will be there one day."

And with that, he resumed his story. As he was saying, the marvel had taken place the day before. The sister had continued the rosary with the same dedication as always, her eyes run through with emotion and her body surrendered to the exalting tension of the supplication. Upon reaching the litanies, the whole convent, including the cook sister, who was away preparing dinner, perceived the imminence of the supernatural in various ways. That is, they knew the miracle was going to happen. The majority of the nuns started to cry for no reason, overcome by an irresistible weeping. Others felt an internal force which caused them to throw themselves onto the floor. They all watched Sister Sabina intently. It was then that God worked through her.

She started by going some two inches up into the air. She was pale and had a pleasant and happy appearance. Then she rose to the head height of the two nuns beside her, the white purity of one of their wimples being dirtied by her shoe, and remained there for a space of time which the sisters estimate could have lasted from three minutes to an hour or an hour and a half. Then, suddenly, as if drawn by a magnet, Sister Sabina set off flying at great speed towards the tabernacle, spun around in two quick and harmonious circles, accidentally put out a candle, and uttering the words, "The enemies of Jesus shall die," fell loudly to the floor. From there, sweaty and exhausted, her sisters picked her up.

The landau's arrival at its destination freed His Excellency from having to discuss a topic which didn't please or impress him in the slightest. He had still barely set foot on the ground, when the slightly glimpsed image of two nuns spying from behind the veils of one of the convent's front windows reminded him that the worry-free happiness of summer was not and would never be for him. He shooed away a curse that peered out of his soul with some Ave Marias, placed himself in God's presence, and briefly meditated on the mystery he was about to celebrate. This helped him to smile at the nuns who were waiting in the doorway to welcome him.

There was a sound of steps and underskirts sliding along corridors, small and anxious voices could be picked up here and there, the indiscreet and rapid closing of doors could be heard, as well as the distressed running of the mother superior, who'd been overly neglectful and hadn't had time to be present at the reception. She kissed his ring faithfully, asked for forgiveness with the red colors of sunset on her face, and brought him to the door of the room for important meetings. His Excellency hurried to take a normal seat, but when he saw the sad eyes of the nun who'd spent the whole day prior sewing and ironing in order to prepare a magnificent episcopal throne made of silks and satins, he stood up again and went to sit with more solemnity. From there he asked if there might be any sick nun, with the intention of visiting her after mass, and he wasn't able to hide his displeasure and his surprise when he heard the mother superior's voice say:

"Sister Sabina, Your Excellency."

He recited another quick and fervent prayer, pulled on the chain of his watch, consulted the time, and headed towards the chapel. The Latin text of the hymn *Veni, Creator Spiritus* restored his happiness, and while putting on his robes at the foot of the altar he thought about how dumb people and bad people are God's children too. With this thought he calmly began, without the anxiety that confronted him at other times, the *Confiteor Deo omnipotenti.*

When he turned around towards the convent to say the first *Dominus vobiscum*, he spotted a nun who walked sort of sliding along the central aisle, held up at the arms by two sisters. Despite the short time that the scene lasted, he was able to engrave the image he'd just seen very clearly inside his head. Pale and unconscious, her eyes veiled by a watery cloud, the sister looked like the living recreation of a *Pietà*. Her left hand resting weakly on her forehead and her right falling fragilely along her emaciated body, both helped to give her an air of shiny and devout enlightenment.

However there was something humorous about the nun's manner that distracted His Excellency and forced him to repeat a few passages from the Canon. Every time he had to turn around for necessities of the ritual, he tried to lower his eyes. On two occasions he even had to bite his lips to suppress a smile. And during communion, when he saw her approach the table, her eyes rolled back into her head and her mouth with an expression of ecstasy, only the seriousness of the moment and the living presence of Sacramental Jesus relieved him from involuntarily revealing what he was thinking about Sister Sabina and her miracles in that moment.

But the nun's presence in the chapel saved him from a visit he didn't desire. That said, upon finishing mass, and anticipating Don Xenaro's efforts to get an aside with the Saint, he hurried not without pangs of regret through the Act of Thanksgiving just to make his hurry more believable when he put it forth as an excuse for not staying afterwards. After having defeated the mother superior's insistence that he take lunch at the convent, seated once again in the landau and looking out the little window at the blue color of the early morning, His Excellency had the feeling he was getting a small taste of the encroaching height of summer.

III

A week had now gone by since Don Xenaro left the most recent report "On Urgent Questions for the Good Governance of the Diocese" on his desk in the study, and he hadn't spoken to him about the topic again since then. The truth is His Excellency was expecting an intervention from his attendant at any moment, and each day that passed without the latter addressing it, he felt an uncomfortable feeling of fear. In any case, the long-awaited conversation couldn't be postponed any further. Signs had been appearing in the air which hinted at such. In the first place, the nun's latest marvel. But above all, the fire in Paris.

It was now four days ago that *El Liberal* had broken the news on its front page. In the Salon des Frères Montreuil in France's capital, the clumsiness of an operator in artlessly handling a film projector had caused a gigantic fire which ended the lives of more than one hundred and thirty viewers in a matter of minutes. The canon theologian had mentioned the incident during the Sunday sermon at the cathedral. He uttered apocalyptic words about that awful tragedy and ended up establishing a convenient and self-interested analogy between the Parisian blaze and the fires of hell. His Excellency understood very well who he was referring to when he spoke about blameworthy tolerance, and what he was actually asking for when he praised the virtue of intolerance, evangelical citations included.

Don Telesforo, the theologian, belonged to Don Xenaro's intimate circle. He was the Saint's confessor, and towards His Excellency he felt a dislike bordering on animosity, which not only did he not bother to hide, but actually tried to display, above all in the clergy offices, where he successfully made jokes at His Excellency's expense. He called him funny nicknames, cast doubt over his knowledge of dogma and morality, and claimed to have a good source in knowing that the bishop had been a mediocre student, most likely a bad one. For his own part, His Excellency felt a confusing feeling of compassion for his thin and elegant theologian, which sometimes turned into forgiveness and other times led to internal laughter, quite especially during the twelve-o'clock Sunday morning sermons when the theologian set himself to nitpicking over whether the Virgin Mary should be considered God-bearer or Christ-bearer.

Now, while His Excellency recited the breviary, he could hear the theologian's careful baritone voice speaking quietly down below with the diocesan judge. If he'd wanted to, he could have ended up overhearing their discussion, word for word. It would have been enough to strain his ears and place himself beside the big stone fireplace, where the words uttered in the offices down below rose up like a tempting, provocative, and strange message, which had nearly reached the point of breaking the bishop's delicate sense of discretion several times. But he resisted. On the other hand he was almost sure he could guess the content of the chatter the two canons were engaged in at that moment: ombre. They both had a passion for gambling.

If Don Telesforo had been in the office next door, in Don Narciso's, the topic of conversation would have been different. A Carlist since his younger days – and he was quickly approaching seventy – the chancellor couldn't live without politics. He'd gone through an anxious and agitated summer, during which, due to doctor's orders, he'd gotten along better with chamomile and lime-blossom tea than with wine. This changed his personality, generally merry and fun by nature, into the attitude of a spiteful, focused, and irritable man. The religious politics of Canalejas – "the liberal jackass," as he called him – put him on the verge of sin everyday just by getting out of bed.

There had been sounds down below throughout the whole morning. Don Narciso's door had been closed angrily at least five times. The printing machines hadn't been on since ten, despite the fact that it was Friday and as such was the last day to run off the fifteen pages of *El testigo de Cristo*. Don Xenaro had frozen all audiences. Don Telesforo was taking too long in the judge's office, and based on the levels of their voices, which had been rising for minutes, the topic couldn't be ombre. His Excellency started to worry.

He closed the breviary and went straight to his desk. He sat down in the large baroque chair, stroked the head of one of the cherubs on which the walnut arms rested, and got ready to plan a defensive strategy for the battle which was doubtlessly being cooked up down below. He grabbed some paper, dipped his pen in the inkwell, turned his eyes towards the vaulted ceiling, and then wrote: "Matter: cinematograph. Not yielding to methods which go against the Gospel. *All things are lawful for me, but all things are not expedient. All things are lawful for me, but all things do not edify. Let no man seek his own, but that which is another's* (Paul, I Cor. 10:22-24)."

23

He stood up and went to see if there was any wine left in the Bargueño desk. There was just a bottle of Calon-Ségur, but that was enough. The others didn't drink. At the most, Don Xenaro was allowed to ask for a tiny pour to wet his cookies, and the theologian refused as a rule whatever His Excellency offered to him, although the latter knew that the canon's mouth watered for Sister Sabina's almond macaroons and that he didn't allow a single one of the pastries which they made for him in the convent to pass by.

He went through his memory to see if he'd forgotten anything, realized everything was settled, breathed deeply, and adjusting his skullcap moved slowly towards the window. He enjoyed looking out between the lace curtains towards the street and the fields. The view offered from there reminded him of the one he could contemplate from the balcony of his house in Mondoñedo. In the distance, above the roofs, the river and poplars. Closer by, a coming and going of people black-clothed and calm, small choruses of priests and canons having a get-together in the middle of the street, and girls and boys toying with hoops and sticks, playing buck buck, or drawing straws for the parts of Cops and Robbers.

He'd gone three years without setting foot in his home town. The trip was long and his mother's death had gotten rid of his desire to go back. He also couldn't leave the diocese in the vicar's hands. Handicapped and sick, foolish in his old age, that man no longer existed to assume any responsibilities. He was the only friend His Excellency had made in the city. Wise and friendly, warm-hearted and cultured, he liked unimportant chitchat and enjoyed the dead hours his ministry left to him. They had both spent beautiful summer afternoons strolling through the palace's vegetable gardens, arm-wrestling with Virgil beneath the lovely shade of the picnic area's trellis, or testing their strength with Sallust's winding prose. Bishop and vicar shared the same passion for literature.

His friend's sickness had been a difficult trial. Deprived of his soothing company and the safety of his advice, His Excellency felt as if abandoned, caught in the misleading trap of appearances and devoured by the teeth of the bright mysticism that surrounded him. For years he'd been the loyal and intelligent collaborator His Excellency needed. A man of faith, always confidently resigned to the act of grace, his support had been as indispensable as it was comforting. He wasn't tricked by the inner voice that pitied him in those depressed moments when he called himself an orphan.

He waited until just before the lunch hour. Some hurried steps up the stone staircase convinced him the moment was approaching, but it didn't take him long to realize it was the palace's servant staff running to help the cook with an urgent last-minute purchase. During the afternoon he began his *sesta* restless and uncomfortable, but in the end was able to sleep. The rest of the afternoon passed silently and in peace.

IV

One day all this calmness started to affect His Excellency on the part of his nerves. An unprovoked and nocturnal diarrhea came to notify him that the past few weeks' tension was going to take its toll. After the mandatory diet imposed by the doctor, he was presented with an unexpected and treacherous loss of appetite which appeared for the first time in front of some salmon patties coated in champignon mushrooms and béchamel sauce, the rejection of which left him sad for several days. Two days later he ordered a marinated cod with raisins and couldn't even cut into it. He tried later on with a cockle pasty and was defeated once more. His Excellency found himself forced to accept that the miseries of the body had also been created for him, and praised God for reminding him of it.

After appetite, it was sleep that escaped. His Excellency spent the nights counting sheep and reciting Ave Marias, pacing around the bedroom and reading thick books which didn't interest him at all. For the first time in many years, he wasn't able to recognize the happiness in the first voices of the day as they multiplied along the streets, the fishwives' singing beneath the window at seven in the morning, offering the fresh fish they'd laid out for the day, the chiming of the bells that woke the city in the four cardinal directions.

Between hunger and sleepiness, the bishop came to realize the summer was nearing its end and he hadn't even made an appearance. He had barely gone out, he'd postponed some visits he tended to make around this time, which always remained as some of the most pleasant memories of the whole year, and he'd been distancing himself far too much from a city and people who in their immense majority, and above all the other virtues, correctly valued that of humility and its correspondence with a plain and good-natured demeanor.

After saying mass alone in the oratory, while redoubling his efforts in front of some chocolate conveniently diluted with water and milk, of which he couldn't even swallow two small baby sips, he decided to spend the whole morning out and about. Beforehand he listened to see what those down below were doing. It seemed that someone was referring to him by the name of Dr. Rhea, although he was unable to figure out what the intent of this joke might be. He heard some soft whispers as if of conspiracy or complicity in Don Narciso's office, and realized the printing press was running again.

In order to go outside, His Excellency chose a cassock without hawser cord, a merino housecoat, a normal hat, and buckleless shoes. He thought that in this way he could easily walk around without being recognized. Then he quickly went down the courtyard's staircase, crossed towards the horse stable, opened the coachman's service door, glanced around carefully to see if there was anyone he knew outside, and left for Arcediagos Street. Out chatting at the entrance to the cathedral were some cassocks which distance and the fear of being discovered prevented him from identifying. He crossed the street to be better protected from the curiosity of the ones talking over there, and went down towards the river.

Walking among the poplars and alders, possibly attracted by the aroma of memories of times past, he felt how his eyes rediscovered an excitement for things, the cleanliness of the air and the satisfied singing of the birds. But not for long, because when he got to the watermill, from the rocky bank he could see the wheel blades stopped and full of reeds and chickweed, and was reminded of his mother's saying: "When the watermill stops, it turns no profit and definitely no crops." Then he veered once more towards the city so as not to pass by the dam, which during those hours he guessed was already full of boys bathing.

In the fields people were busy harvesting potatoes. Each time the hoe entered the ground and uprooted the tucked-away fruit, His Excellency experienced the dusty and vegetative enjoyment present in farmers when they verified the sure presence of that buried treasure. Some of them were singing. The children were messing around here and there, and the women were following behind the men with baskets in their hands, bent over the open furrows, collecting the potatoes to be eaten and setting aside those to be replanted. The sun was getting hot, and an alarming blackness of thunderclouds hovered over the mountaintops to the south.

The year before had been a bad one. A dry winter, rich only in colds and frosts, had brought hunger. A ghostly mob of ragged men and women had come down from the mountains and invaded the city. They had settled in the arcades of Constitution Square, with the old people and children laid out on the ground, shut up in a dramatic silence, stretching out their pleading hands towards the people who walked by. His Excellency had ordered for a couple of cows to be bought and slaughtered and had done everything possible to contribute to the disaster relief, but circumstances had overwhelmed his personal goodwill. Seeing people digging in the earth now, he felt within himself the warm murmur of a human joy he shared.

Upon arriving at the Bridge of the Revolting Crime, the bishop stopped to say a prayer for the victims of the latest Carlist uprising. Seven of the city's residents – a lawyer, two working girls, a carpenter, a shoemaker, and two peasants – had been barbarically murdered here. Taken from their homes under cover of night, they had suffered horrible torments before dying. Two of them had had their eyes plucked out while still alive, the women had had their breasts chopped off, and one of the peasants had had his head caved in by rifle butts… They turned up the next day hanging from the bridge's largest arch. Ever since then some men preferred to cross the river further down, above the dry boulders of the dam.

Turning down the Lady's Track towards the terraces of the Alameda, His Excellency was thinking about old readings. He couldn't look back on the First Book of the Maccabees without an internal tremor. He wasn't affected so much by the unending list of crimes recounted there – disemboweled women, children hung by their necks, men with their throats slit… – as by the list of orders and prohibitions that had triggered so much blood: the abolition of holy sacrifices, the profanation of the sabbath, the contamination of sanctuaries, and the slaughter of pigs and impure animals. The reading of verse 52 in particular had caused him physical discomfort ever since his days as a student of Scripture: *And that whosoever would not do according to the word of king Antiochus should be put to death.*

He preferred the overjoyed and pagan nectar of the Song of Songs, its flavor like good-tasting wine, the wide palate of its verses. The memory of Don Epifanio Estévez, a role model for confessors in his Mondoñedo seminary, always came to his mind in moments like that. Climbing the hill, he remembered this man's maxims: "Better a slacker than a fanatic," "Goodness always over justice," "Christ on the cross before Christ with the whip"... Amid the muffled cries of boys bathing in the river, a deep and placid aroma reached His Excellency. He used this opportunity to take a break and look around calmly.

To his right, on the outskirts of the city, in the upper Vilachá neighborhood, half isolated among cob shacks, the Barbagelatta cinema. Over its roof, a green and white flag. It was a sign. On Sunday afternoons, from the window in the palace office a flood of people could be seen going up Pote Street to flow, curious and festive, onto the Royal Road. There they would wait, sometimes for more than an hour, for the doors to open. Then they would jam against one another, as if a necessity long delayed had suddenly become imperative and priceless.

With a smile on his lips, His Excellency continued his stroll. The sun burned strongly. The rising and falling of hoes on the ground was calmer now. He retraced his steps and went down once more to the riverbank. From a crack between two boulders arose some water that the bishop knew very well. He rolled his cassock up to his waist, stepped firmly onto the tip of a rock which served as a step to reach the height of the fountainhead, bent over as far as he could, and started to lap up the water. The freshness that filled first his mouth and then his throat momentarily transported him to a faraway playground of woodlands and meadows. With this pleasant feeling in his body, he began his walk back.

V

That morning at mass he prayed for his enemies, and during the *Memento* the Gethsemane scene passed through his head like a lightning bolt, with Jesus anguished and dripping blood, begging the Father for help in such a dire moment. Then he reflected for half an hour on the mystery of the cross and felt an almost violent desire to confess himself. In truth he didn't really know if what he wanted was to enjoy the comforting grace of reconciliation or to simply be listened to, to confide in someone. He went over to the cathedral through the courtyard, stood on the tips of his toes to see if the confessor was free, and there he went, shadow among other shadows, to fall down on his knees before him.

The confessor was a little ninety-two-year-old man, wise and kind, who had the habit of placing his sharp and cold nose on one's left ear during confession. He lived in solitude, preparing his dinners in the ascetic discomfort of a small and dark room he occupied in the upper part of the cathedral, and only received the isolated and secret visit of some great sinner, who came to seek forgiveness and consolation. He smiled at everyone and tended to say that as far as sins were concerned exaggeration was a problem. He considered Don Telesforo to be overly impulsive and a bit too wrapped up in his books. Regarding Sister Sabina he thought she needed a good yank on the ears.

His Excellency left from there with an internal strength he hadn't had for a while. He ran into the palace's coachman shoeing the gray riding horse on the patio and stopped to chat with him. Then he went up to the dining room and ate a leisurely lunch, drank a glass of tonic wine, and rang the little silver bell so they would bring him the day's press. They handed him *La Verdad* and *El Liberal*, the latter without its title, following a custom established by his predecessor, who'd ordered them to cut the front headline from that newspaper with scissors before bringing it to him. Romanones remained insistent that the teaching staff of religious schools needed to have academic certification in line with that of public institutes. *La Verdad* dedicated its front page to the same topic, and between the needles of a flowery and sharp verbiage the bishop was able to discern his theologian's cold, shortsighted eyes.

Truthfully the law didn't seem so bad to him, although there were two aspects of it he wasn't exactly pleased by. In the first place its cloudy motivation. It was obvious that what this sly Romanones was trying to do was curb the growing prestige of Canalejas, who by raising the anticlerical banner was attracting even the moderate liberal sympathies towards his positions. That is, he wanted to play with the interests of the Church in order to solve the party's internal problems. A sin fell out of his mouth here and he didn't bother to restrain it or sanitize it with quick and fervent prayers. He let it fly freely with express dedication towards the politician.

But what's more, the law transgressed in another way. By not granting a time frame for the affected staff to be able to adjust to the situation, he committed a clear injustice. Now then, putting aside the two flaws, the rest of it didn't scare His Excellency. Why refuse an unofficial inspection of educational institutes by the Ministry of Public Education? Why wouldn't principals have to be responsible for whatever is said or taught in those schools which goes against the civil and political order of the State?

He put the newspaper down for a moment, took out the pencil from his cassock's inside pocket, and wrote in his notebook: "Matter: Romanones decree. Defending the rights of the Church. Trust and faith. *Who walk to go down into Egypt, and have not asked at my mouth, hoping for help in the strength of Pharao, and trusting in the shadow of Egypt. And the strength of Pharao shall be to your confusion, and the confidence of the shadow of Egypt to your shame* (Isaiah 30:2-3)." He looked over what he'd written, left the notebook on top of the desk, put away the pencil, and continued to read the newspaper.

El Liberal dedicated an article on its inside pages to Sister Sabina and her levitation. It was signed by Kepler. His Excellency stopped for a moment to think who could be hiding behind that pseudonym, but he quickly realized that without reading the article first, the game would be too difficult. When he had gotten through three lines, he'd already eliminated the editor of the newspaper. Eight lines in, he began to suspect the Professor of Physics at the Provincial Education Institute, a furious Voltairean embittered by an unrequited love. After fifteen, he felt sure about his suspicion. By the end he had irrefutable evidence that he was right.

Kepler began his article, written in Castilian, by alluding to a "certain unhealthy cave in our city which serves as a refuge for feminine frustrations, and that if the basic sanitary norms which governed other countries were to govern ours, would be shut down for simple reasons of hygiene – spiritual and… the other kind." Of course, the author was referring to the convent. Next up was a comparison between Spain and Africa, "the continent where every superstition has its place," and a reflection on what characterizes the most advanced societies and what differentiates them from the most backwards. "Reason is the key to this mess," he declared.

Sister Sabina appeared named as an ignorant and self-interested swindler, love child "of the marriage between irrationality and misery, and sister to error, stupidity, and wickedness." Then came the body of the argument and the central part of the article: as against levitation, the theory of universal gravitation. After expounding upon the basics of Newton's physics, with long-winded digressions on mass, distance, and constants, Kepler finished by saying: "To pretend, when we have just inaugurated the twentieth century, that a human being can by his own means remove himself from the forces of gravity is a task as vain as it is ridiculous. To denounce an imposter is our duty as men of Science and lovers of Progress."

His Excellency enjoyed imagining the controversy to come. He could see the theologian on his way to the seminary to consult with the teacher of the discipline, in search of arguments that would demonstrate the scientific possibility of the miracle. It wasn't hard for him to get inside his canon's head to witness the construction of his intellectual framework. No citation of the Sacred Scriptures, not even a single word taken from the Gospels of Jesus.

Convoluted historical reflections on the position of popes towards Science. Relativization of human knowledge. Invocation of Primary and secondary causes…

More than ever, that morning the bishop regretted the enforced absence of his vicar. It also wasn't hard for him to imagine the vicar's friendly smile and the intelligent irony of his sharp commentaries on Kepler's article. What wouldn't have occurred to that caustic genius about the subjects in question! What a heap of playful sayings about that fool's scientific, clerical, and reverential hypocrisies! As a homage to the friend crucified by sickness in his bed, His Excellency thought about writing a blind man's ballad titled, "To Be a Priest Without Knowing It, or How to Recite Prose Thinking That One Is Reciting Poetry and Verse." A couple of octameters to begin with even occurred to him, but he threw them out for being too mischievous and profane.

The current events page was pierced, scintillating and tense, by the shadow of Cain. In the parish of Vilar de Santos, Pedro Barrio, native resident of the area, fifty years old, castrator by profession, unmarried, had been detained by the Patrol accused of being guilty of the death of his brother Paco, forty-eight, father of five children, blacksmith by trade, resident of the same parish, with a house in the Casás area. The motive: disagreements over shares. The weapon: a pig-slaughtering knife. Circumstances: by night, at a crossroads. Twenty-seven stabs. One of them straight and clean right into the center of his heart

Before turning the page, His Excellency had a thought for the little orphan children and a feeling of justice and pity for the fratricide. He thought about saving a small slot for the death at the next day's mass. And as if to soften things, upon flipping the page, a kind of sketch. The teacher from the co-ed school in Sarois had bitten the ear of the village mayor, whose auditory appendix had gotten stuck between his attacker's teeth. The latter ran away in a hurry with his prize and locked himself in his house with keys and bars. Clamor and indignation from the neighbors. Rocks against the door. Shouts for him to give up the ear. Inside, silence. At last the serene and peaceful words of an old patriarch, with centuries of humanity hanging off the plea, and a window that opens. Anticipation and silence. The ear comes flying through the air and lands in some blackberry bushes. A dog ran faster than the boys who ran to look for it.

His Excellency's laugh began under his breath as a prayer. Then he remained stuck in breathless respiration for a few moments, and finally exploded like a rowdy line of cannons. He had to hold his stomach with his hands, to throw back his head, and wasn't at ease until a flood of sobs and tears dragged out a dark and murky river of many days, possibly of many years.

VI

He went towards the closet, opened the door, and looked for the clothes he needed. There was an abundance of shirts and pants, but not a single jacket. This small setback lit up a brief doubt in his head, but the memory of the summer and the possibility of going out in light clothing made his mind up for him in choosing a button-up cardigan which he used during the winter to put over his cassock when he was working. He dressed quickly, covered his head with a cap, and went half sneakily into the corridor. There was nobody around. He went down the stone staircase to the courtyard, slid along the wall, and entered the horse stable. Glued to the door that led out onto the street, he waited for the footsteps of someone who'd just walked in front to pass by. Then he opened it with care, looked cautiously to his right and left, and went out.

He laughed at himself as he walked along the street, wondering what he must look like to the people whose paths he crossed. Maybe he had the appearance of an unimportant businessman or a villager on a night-time visit to the capital. Upon arriving at Leña Square, he turned down below the arcades towards the Alameda, trying to get as far away as possible from Danger Alley, even though he'd have to go quite out of his way for that. Passing in front of a bakery, the smell of octopus pasties reminded him of the tragedy of a faraway appetite which still hadn't come back, and he felt even more justified in the adventure he was about to set out on. Some guards said good evening without recognizing him.

Now at the doors to the Barbagelatta cinema he was at the point of turning back. The number of people going in, the noise of the piano being played inside, the hot and sticky clamor coming out of the door in dizzying stenches all weakened his resolve a bit. He thought about the scandal which could ensue if someone identified him, about the myth which would be used to deform reality, about the opportunity he was going to place in the palms of his enemies' hands. In order to prevent his doubts from growing and his indecisiveness from turning into fear, he started to walk towards the door. An extremely thin, almost skeletal, little man with a big waxy mustachio and a goatee stopped him:

"Signore, it's five *chéntimos*," he said as he blocked the path.

His Excellency searched in his pocket, took out a *real*, and dropped it into the Italian's gnarled hand. He entered the big hut with his head down. He immediately realized none of his worry was justified. In the first place, the light which lit up the inside was so slight that anything just six feet away could barely be seen. Additionally, the commotion which was going on inside, from the unrestrained shouts to the foaming language, pointed towards an audience he assumed wouldn't know him. He found an empty spot and sat down. In the shadows he frightfully discovered some eyes that were looking at him intensely, and he felt discovered. But he quickly realized the look carried a different meaning: the one who was looking ended up changing seats with his wife, whom he placed far from the bishop, right next to the central aisle.

It was obvious that the hut, with its dirt floor, had once been an ancient furnace. Against the back, fastened to a beam by some ropes, hung an old, somewhat yellow linen sheet. To the right stood a small platform made of boxes half-hidden by a discolored Spanish flag, and on the other side, its back to the benches occupied by the audience, an old piano. It was being played without much enthusiasm by a thin, somewhat hunchbacked woman, who occasionally cast a glance at the little boy sleeping in a cot at her feet. Tied to one of the piano's legs, a small dog, scruffy and unclean.

To His Excellency's left, just next to the woman who'd changed seats at her husband's command, stood the short body of an old china cabinet missing its drawers and doors. Above it, a huge wooden box painted black from which sprouted a crank. In front, facing towards the sheet, a metal tube on the ends of which the name "Lumière" could be read in large letters. A group of four men, with their hands in their pockets and their bodies arched forwards, gestured at the machine and commented and conjectured about the secrets and intricacies of its inner workings.

When His Excellency was starting to worry about the delay, behind him, as if reading his mind, a group of boys began to shout, "Barbagelatta, don't act like nothing's the matta!" Further away, a forty-or-so-year-old man, with a cap and a butcher's smock on, was beating the head of his cane against a bench and shouting unintelligible comments towards the woman at the piano. The dog was barking.

Three boys who looked like rich students were throwing rocks against the linen cloth. A colossal fart, coming from one of the benches at the back, caused a collective burst of laughter which His Excellency joined enthusiastically.

It was then that the man from the door approached, clapping his hands and pleading for silence. Without breaking off his speech, he put on a jacket hanging in a crevice of the wall and got up onto the platform in one hop. From there, requesting silence once more with a movement of his hands, he said:

"Signoras and signores, what we are going to see here this evening is an incomparibile espectacle. The device which you may all observare en fronte of your eyes, invented by the prophets, Auguste and Louis Lumière de Paris, permits the collezione, in a serie of instantes proofs, of all the movements that durante a certain periodo of time occur en fronte of the machine, and reproduces these movements continuamente by projecting its immagines in a naturale size onto a screen and before an entire room."

Mr. Barbagelatta's speech was received by whistles and cries of approval, which he accepted with satisfaction, only to continue:

"And now a breve announcement. The danger that is run by manipulare the carbide lampara that makes this maraviglia possible, obligates this operatore to a concentrazione which would be impossibile in the mezzo of the noise that dominates the room. Because of this, to evoid an accidente mortale I ask for a silenzio absoluto, as if you were all en a church."

A collective murmur signed off on the words of the Italian, who got down from the platform with a learned seriousness, making his way theatrically towards the machine's location. There he got onto a small stool to dim the lamp which lit up the hut, and the small clamor that began in the darkness was immediately hushed by the disapproving shushes of the rest. A sharp and humorous statement about the Italian woman's hunchback froze in the air without a response. The excitement in the room also entered His Excellency's heart, which started to beat faster.

And all of a sudden, the marvel. A locomotive shooting into the room at full speed caused panic and chaos. People began to run and scream. Some tried to open the door. The women were crying. The butcher had hidden himself under the bench. The dog was barking. An old man was calling for help. During the two minutes the film projection lasted, the room had turned into a kind of fair, in which it was impossible to pay attention to the images being reflected on the sheet. When the light came on again in the middle of that enormous clamor, Barbagelatta was able to convince the audience not without effort that everything was fine and everyone should return to their seats. Then, without losing his theatrical composure for a second, he asked forgiveness, reciting the following words from his heart:

"It was a serious errore, an unforgivable errore mio, to not warn the pubblico that today we are honored by the presenza, of the realismo of the immagines we were going to see. I ask your pardono. Never again will we fall into such dangerous procedere. And now, my apolochies given, my cultured espectators, we will continuare with the sessione, with the incentivo addizionale, per which I give my word, that there will be no more unpleasant things to observare."

Afterwards, in the silence Barbagelatta had achieved with his plea from the beginning, came a movie about worshippers leaving the noon mass at Zaragoza's Basilica of Our Lady of the Pillar, another about worshippers leaving the Church of Santa María de Sans, in Barcelona, one more about workers leaving a factory, and lastly a documentary about the burial of Pope Leo XIII. At the end, Barbagelatta got onto the stage again, thanked those attending for their exemplary behavior, and said that as a reward he and his wife would perform a short Italian farewell ballad.

His Excellency got up then and went towards the door to avoid the crowds at the end. He stood there waiting for the event to end and afterwards, with his cap pulled all the way down to his ears, headed back. He returned the way he'd come. Upon passing in front of the Franciscan church he couldn't avoid the almost mechanical gesture of making the sign of the cross. He looked around to make sure he hadn't been discovered, and with his hands stuck in his pockets sank into the protective darkness of Paxaros Street.

Back in the palace, as he took notes about what he'd just seen, still with the excitement in his eyes and chest, he felt his runaway appetite announce its return in a violent and demanding way. There were a couple bars of chocolate, but he had to give mass the next day.

VII

The surprise of running into the canon penitentiary there ended up unexpectedly altering the blueprints His Excellency had been outlining for the past few days. Apparently, those below had expanded their circle of influence further than he'd been able to imagine from the isolated solitude of his office. He glanced sidelong at Don Telesforo and discovered the satisfied happiness of triumph on his face. Don Narciso seemed at ease, possibly convinced the meeting was going to be a pure formality. The attendant, on the other hand, was trying to reconcile a kind of devoted submission to his master with the moral rigidity that demanded loyalty to his colleagues. His mouth smiled, but those eyes had a suspicious and guilty look to them, as if he could perceive the resentment towards him which was nestled in His Excellency's heart.

The dean was there too. Weak in soul and body, his spirit permanently divided between fear and obedience, he avoided looking forward and was half hidden behind Don Xenaro's bulky anatomy. Not counting the old, the sick, and the indifferent, only the diocesan judge was missing. That was no mistake. The conversation between the latter and Don Telesforo in the past few days, raised in tone and agitated, had obviously not been about ombre. That said, the bishop hadn't come to understand what the reasons could be for this unexpected loyalty on the part of a man who had until then shown little interest in issues of diocesan governance.

The first to speak was Don Xenaro. Waving those white and chubby hands that made His Excellency think about the somewhat meaty softness of his tender spirit, he said:

"If Your Excellency will allow it, we would like to express our concern over some issues related to morality and good practice."

"Go ahead, my children," the bishop responded with an impersonal and dry voice, drained of all affection and wanting to appear firm.

Don Xenaro, incapable of interpreting the hidden subtleties of that voice, stutteringly hesitated and rushed to give his turn to Don Telesforo, who was seated to his right and continued to stare fixedly and calmly at the prelatial table, behind which the bishop entrenched himself at a defensive and hierarchically calculated distance. For a few moments, bishop and canon challenged one another with their eyes, but the theologian's stubborn and cold determination was more powerful than the prelate's pride and his condescending mask. When the latter turned his gaze through the window towards the poplars by the river, Don Telesforo took the floor.

"The truth is we would like to know Your Honor's opinion in relation to the most recent report on urgent questions for the good governance of the diocese."

"Is the honorable theologian referring to the matter of the cinematograph?" asked the bishop.

This question didn't need an answer. Only Don Xenaro nodded his head in affirmation. The rest remained intent on His Excellency, who added:

"I wanted to hear your impressions first."

"We believe that…"

His Excellency interrupted the theologian with a movement of his hand.

"If you don't mind, I would like to know my dear confessor's opinion first," he said. And with a sarcasm he didn't bother to hide, he added:

"Saintliness and experience should come with preferential treatment."

Don Telesforo received the blow without any external sign that might indicate the violence which had doubtlessly just erupted within him. He moved his gaze away from His Excellency and turned to look at the canon penitentiary.

"I," said the little old man smiling and hardly even raising his voice, "have little opinion to offer. I no longer go out on the street and am ignorant of the things which occur in the city. I would like to have information that in this moment I do not possess. I believe the honorable theologian, who has studied the topic, should have informed the rest of us beforehand so that we could have formed a fair and well-founded opinion."

The confessor's words brought light back to the bishop's dim eyes. With a friendlier and less rigid voice than at the beginning, he directed himself towards Don Narciso:

"And what is the honorable chancellor's impression?"

The response came quickly and without formality:

"That this disgrace is intolerable!"

It was the signal. Don Telesforo resolutely took out the papers he'd held in his hand since the beginning, and without waiting for any kind of indication from the bishop, began to speak:

"I shall read a report prepared by four theologians of known expertise and proven virtue."

"Might their names be known?"

"They prefer to remain anonymous," the canon responded.

"In any case," interjected the penitentiary, "if you all will allow me a few words, I would dare say that our dear prelate is right. It is not proper to hide from him of all people the names of four competent priests of the diocese he governs."

The bishop looked gratefully at the man, and as if this intervention had left him satisfied, limited himself to indicating:

"In order to avoid misinterpretations, we'll leave it as it is. However I would like it to be clear to the honorable theologian that I'm voluntarily giving up a right which is afforded to me as bishop."

"I personally think that the serious issue which brings us here has nothing to do with a matter which remains incidental," Don Telesforo abbreviated, already uncomfortable from so much delay.

"Move on then," indicated His Excellency.

The report consisted of four parts written in Castilian. The first contained a clear and detailed description of the Lumière brothers' invention: the optical-chemical procedure of the reproduction of static reality, the theory of persistence of vision by the physician Peter Mark Roget, the function of the Geneva drive or Maltese cross tasked with intermittent rotary motion... There followed a brief history of the cinematograph, in which the recurring theme of detracting from the French inventors' merit was developed by diluting them within a nebula of conjoining inventions, among which were cited the fathers of the magic lantern, the fantascope, the zoetrope, the stroboscope, the photographic gun, and the kinetoscope.

The third part was dedicated to telling of the material damages caused by the invention, among which had to be counted at least seventy fires, some of them with deaths and injuries, which the high flammability of the celluloid film in use suggested were going to continue. A passing reference to the Fourth Commandment and to the grave sin committed by those who carelessly put life itself at risk anticipated the doctrinal content reserved for the fourth part. But before that appeared an expert's report written by a Madrid ophthalmologist about the ailments which can arise in the sight of people who attend the spectacle, and a general practitioner's justified doubts about the damaging influences which could be had on the human brain from the rapid projection of a series of discontinuous images.

The four theologians concluded their study by referring to the spiritually harmful aspects of the invention in question. The cinematograph, which was also discredited from an aesthetic point of view ("a carnival attraction and lacking in taste"), produced a loosening of willpower, clouded one's capacity for judgment, and created the illusion and the enchantment of a false reality. What's more, the darkness which was necessary to carry out the projection lent itself to sinful excesses easily imaginable for anyone. In this respect there were reliable reports, which a basic sense of discretion suggested not be made explicit, that in the city's Barbagelatta cinema situations had arisen which a simple reference to the word "orgy" described only roughly and with some indulgence.

In the final part, the theologians gathered news and rumors about certain films that had already been played abroad which included filth and indecency, and they speculated about the future. They imagined the city overflowing with caves like the one that already existed, crowds piling in front of the doors, fighting to get in, families destroyed, teens stupefied, children prematurely chained to this new vice, robberies and assaults in order to be able to buy a ticket...

The report, read by the canon theologian in a deliberate and firm voice, from which registers of a certain bright and messianic theatricality were not absent, was received with an uncomfortable silence. Don Xenaro gazed sorrowfully at the floor.

The dean had signs of concern and anguish engraved on his face. Don Narciso waited. His Excellency observed them all, one by one. They seemed to him like enormous pictures in an abandoned oratory. Spread above them was something like an ancestral layer of blue powder, of time never regained, of rotten and ailing air. Only the confessor's serene old age gave a human touch to that assembly of ghosts.

Don Telesforo spoke first:

"Our duty is complete."

Before answering him, the bishop looked anxiously at the vaulted ceiling, as if searching for an air that he lacked. Then he said:

"Mine as well."

And with that, he stood up and put out his ring for them to kiss. He accompanied them to the door and watched them disappear, their heads drooping and all the anguish in the world hanging like a coat on their backs, into the old and damp darkness of the palace. His Excellency returned to his desk, took some notes, sprinkled some pounce over the fresh ink, and made his way towards the window. The sun marked the exact point of noon in the sky. Several officials from the Tax Ministry, formal and bearded, were chatting outside the Municipal Office, on the sidewalk out front, just on the corner of Ponte Street. A cart full of watermelons passed by. Marching alongside the palace wall, hurried and tragic, was the disquieting shadow of the theologian.

VIII

His Excellency received the news that Sister Sabina was waiting in the antechamber without the excitement Don Xenaro's words apparently wished to achieve with the simple announcement of said visit. With his eyes lost in the brightness of the recently opened window, he asked his attendant about the rest of the audiences for the morning, wanted to confirm a couple pieces of information beforehand about economic issues related to the Seminary's pantry, and gave him orders that the landau be prepared for the early hours of the afternoon: he was going to the hospital to visit the sick. Then he said:

"Have Sister Sabina come in."

The nun, deep dark bags under her eyes and extremely pale cheeks, entered as if sliding through the air, hardly even grazing the floor. A starchy white noise accompanied the sister's elegant genuflection upon planting herself in front of the bishop to kiss his ring. She requested to remain on her knees for the rest of the audience, but His Excellency helped her to stand up and take the violet armchair in the back corner, where he spoke with visitors. Sister Sabina protested with a barely perceptible wrinkling, half frown and half smile, and without any more resistance she seated herself in the place His Excellency had indicated. She carried a rosary in her hand and stared chastely at an undefined point in the back of the room, avoiding a clash of her faint and blue gaze against the prelate's resolute one.

It was the first time His Excellency had found himself alone with her, without the beatified and reverent company of her sisters in religion, before the easy and submissive admiration of Don Xenaro or the attentive and watchful expectancy of the theologian. Seated in front of him, with her delicate hands lost in the protective shelter of the insides of a visibly starched habit, the nun seemed smaller, thinner, and more fragile than he'd always thought. But at the same time, from beneath her transparent skin exited something like a powerful and blood-red ebullition which His Excellency was forced to distance from himself in order not to fall into its charm. For the first time in the fifteen long years he'd been at the head of the diocese, he didn't dare to mentally discredit Sister Sabina with the ease and the lack of doubt with which he had done up until then. And even without allowing himself to be affected by her charisma, he thought how that person right there was at least worthy of respect.

And in this way he prepared himself to listen to her. Not even the long circumlocution she made before getting directly into the topic which had brought her to the palace, and in which he sensed the influence of the nun's confessor, managed to irritate His Excellency, always on guard with people incapable of saying things quickly and to the point. He forgave her by thinking about the nervousness she must have felt from the simple act of daring to pass through those doors, and the image of the sister flying through the air, which in other moments would have provoked a humorous thought for him, ended up interesting him even more in the purposes which had brought her before him. As if sensing what he was thinking about in that moment, Sister Sabina said:

"Your Excellency must realize this conversation is not easy for me…"

Bending his head in a way which sought to be an invitation to trust, the bishop answered:

"I'm aware of that, my daughter. Of course I'm aware of that."

Sister Sabina took her hands out from under her habit, laced them together nervously, gazed at His Excellency's curious and peaceful eyes, and continued:

"The tasks which the Lord entrusts to us are not always pleasant."

"Tell me without fear what he asks of you on this occasion."

"He commands me to safeguard the salvation of Your Excellency's soul."

"Is it in such danger?" the bishop asked smiling.

As an answer, Sister Sabina broke into tears, assaulted all of a sudden by a sorrow without consolation. The sobbing was so intense that her tiny body was shaken by rapid and growing convulsions, as if the force which came out of her fragile wax skin was rearing up and threatening to completely overflow right there, without respect for either manners or conventions. His Excellency was paralyzed, surprised by a reaction he hadn't counted on, and a cold that climbed up from some dark and secret region of his heart froze the words in his throat.

When the shock had finally been recovered from, he moved his round right hand, on which was displayed the careful tidiness of some bright and polished fingernails, and slowly placed it on the sister's forearm. The latter, continuing to cry, fell to her knees and began to cover him with kisses and tears. The whiteness and the paleness of her lips contrasted with the heat that burned within them and which penetrated disturbingly into His Excellency's body. And while she kissed his hand, incapable of containing the sobs drowning her, Sister Sabina continued to say with the same passion:

"Your Excellency must to do something for his soul! Your Excellency must do something for his soul!"

His Excellency was then able to speak:

"Calm down, calm down. My soul rests in the Lord's merciful hands."

Then he stood up, made an effort for the nun to copy his example, and both of them once again occupied the chairs where they'd sat before. His Excellency, calm restored, without a display of concern on his once again peaceful face, tried to pacify the nun. He shook the little silver bell, silently awaited the servant, who didn't take long to arrive, and made his request:

"Have them prepare a linden tea."

And without giving Sister Sabina a chance to protest, he added:

"Bring a couple of snacks too."

Still tearful, the nun began a movement of protest on her lips which the bishop quickly cut off:

"You already know what Saint Teresa says about pouting. I have a nicely cured ham that brightens even the heart. With fresh bread from the *Canóniga* bakery and a little glass of wine, it will help us see things more calmly right away."

"I'm not in the habit," said Sister Sabina. "Also," she added, "I'm sure my confessor would chastise me for it."

"When the Lord created man he dignified all the things in this world. Jesus ate."

"And fasted," the sister boldly pointed out.

"But fasting was the exception. Hunger opens the doors of the soul to pessimism and sadness. And from there oftentimes to the devil."

The nun's face turned intensely red. His Excellency then realized he might be wounding deeply held feelings and no longer persisted in the topic. When the servant left the requested tray on the coffee table, the bishop respected Sister Sabina's decision not to try a mouthful, not even the warm water of the tea, which remained steaming in the china cup for the rest of the audience.

"Your confessor should be a bit less rigid with you," said the bishop.

Sister Sabina's eyes became dark all of a sudden. Her face's red color was turning once again to the nunlike paleness that her cheeks had shown at the beginning. A facial rigidity, enraged and violent, translated the internal tension which brought her to angrily clench her jaw. Something like a metallic ray of light left her eyes and crashed against His Excellency's forehead.

"My confessor," she said in a voice that concealed a scream, "is a good minister to the Lord who knows how to do his duty."

"I didn't say he wasn't," apologized the bishop.

"If his advice were listened to more often, we would not be seeing the scandals in this diocese which cause the Lord our God to suffer so much."

His Excellency made an effort not to lose his calm:

"In truth I'm perfectly happy with the members of my diocese. I have nothing in particular to complain about."

"There has never been so much sin. The Lord suffers."

Without responding to the nun's last words, the bishop demanded his attendant's presence. Don Xenaro was there in an instant.

"Accompany Sister Sabina, please."

He got to his feet and allowed the sister to kiss his ring. He then asked her to keep him in her prayers and tried to be a bit more than polite in his farewell. The nun left crying. His Excellency kept the door open until he saw her reach the main staircase. She was walking hurriedly. From there she turned around to look. The sadness, maybe the infinite sorrow which languished in her eyes at that moment, made the hundred-year-old darkness inside the bishop's palace even gloomier.

IX

He rushed through the Angelus prayer thinking about the pleasure of reading which awaited him. His Excellency felt a gluttonous anxiety towards newspapers and magazines, an exciting curiosity that provided him with secret joys. Sometimes he even put the moment off in order to prolong the pleasant feeling, in the same way that he had the habit of leaving the most appetizing bite on the side of his plate, which he then consumed at the end with an unhurried and conscious delight. The newspaper hour was one of the most beautiful hours of the day. He delayed it until mid-morning so it would coincide with breakfast: fresh bread and slices of stiff ham with a tiny bit of Amandi red wine. At eleven thirty on the dot what invariably took place was something which was a kind of daily and domestic miracle for him.

When the servant reverentially departed from the office, after leaving the small silver tray on top of the marble centerpiece where *El testigo de Cristo* was awaiting, His Excellency let himself fall, curious and happy, into the eighteenth-century armchair, upholstered in fabric, which he used on these occasions. He heard animated voices in the area below, among which he could make out those of the theologian and the diocesan judge. He forgot about them without much effort and started to read.

The first page was taken up almost entirely by a photo of Sister Sabina, in which the nun, with a tormented and somber expression, gazed at an image of the Christ of Limpias. A calculated combination of lights and shadows added veiled hints of prophetic anguish to the sister's tragic face. The gleam of faith shone in her eyes, and behind it could be perceived a bold and resolute determination which awoke old fears in His Excellency's tranquil soul.

However the caption in Castilian describing the photo provoked a smile on the prelate's serious face: "A heart for Christ. A couple of blue eyes for faith. A dove for the Church. Sister Sabina Reverter." He knew the hand responsible very well. Having just arrived in the diocese, when discussing the contents of *El testigo de Cristo* entry by entry and chapter by chapter with Don Xenaro, his attendant's colorful prose had almost always turned out to be an unassailable stronghold. Even after a general substitution of adjectives and nouns and the merciless elimination of asides and parentheses, an unpredictable and floaty poetic debris remained, which lent the whole journal an air of something white, mushy, and feminine.

However in the article which was included in the "De Historia Ecclesiae" section there throbbed a beat of a different thickness. The good rhetorical training of the theologian, a scholastic as logical as he was focused, without rejecting the flourishes of a language sensitive to congratulations and praises, attempted not to neglect values which he considered to be far above his personal brilliance and which were never lacking in his writings. On this occasion, the topic was the papal crisis during the so-called Babylonian Captivity.

An experience which was now many years old advised His Excellency to read all of the articles carrying his theologian's signature at their foot, carefully and several times over. He then grabbed his pen and began to underline any ideas, words, or pieces of information that drew his attention for any reason. The first lines concerned the much-adored names of Saint Brigid and Saint Catherine of Siena, both censured for their conduct by the Avignon popes, whom they repeatedly urged to return to the abandoned city. The adjectives dedicated to these two women were equally worthy of the bishop's interest: *courageous, bold, saintly, rebellious, fulfillers of an unpleasant task...*

In the biographical note about Cardinal Baldassarre Cossa, the one who rose to the papal throne in 1410 with the name of John XXIII and who'd been a pirate and a bandit, His Excellency underlined the Castilian sentence: "Not even the Papacy escaped from the indignity of some of its members." When he finished, he had to place himself in God's presence in order not to curse the theologian. But displeasure quickly crumbled after reading what he said about the Cretan Petros Philargos, pope in 1409 with the name of Alexander V. He called him a "hedonist" four times in five lines without being redundant and employed sarcasm to refer to his well-known affection for good wine. He listed some of the gems which could be found in his famous Avignon wine cellar, and finished by speculating without much sharpness on the value of sacrifice. However not a single word alluding to the evangelical generosity and the human refinement of that great pontiff.

Turning the page, he heard the increasingly animated voice of the article's author down below, and couldn't avoid the comical act of raising his glass in the air as a toast. Then he stopped at the contribution signed by Don Xenaro and hesitated for a moment, but the first words of the document, more glimpsed than actually read, began to nudge at his curiosity. It dealt with a vision the nun had had a few days ago, during which the Lord had given her important revelations about the other life. Like Saint Teresa, Sister Sabina had attained the grace of seeing souls snow over hell, flakes and more flakes falling endlessly into Satan's terrifying kingdom.

It had happened at night, while the Saint was praying in front of the Monstrance. Suddenly the Sacramental bread had started to grow... And it grew so much that it ended up filling up the whole front of the chapel, covering the high altar and the altarpiece. Then, the image of Christ crucified and agonizing appeared above the immaculate color of the host. He was white and thin, with his head bent over his chest, which rose and fell at a slow, almost eternal pace. From that tragic position he looked at her with a lost and weak gaze, one of infinite anguish. He moved his lips, let a terrifying whimper escape, and from the same spot of his mouth emerged a tiny black dot which, little by little, in concentric circles, came to cover the whole white surface of the Sacramental bread.

Some short tongues of flame then appeared along the area below. An unbearable heat, suffocating and rotten, started to fill the church all of a sudden. It was then that snowflakes began to fall from the area above. Millions of them for a long time, possibly hours, as they found the sister unconscious the next day upon going down for mass, stretched out along the floor, belly down and drenched in sweat and water.

The reading finished, His Excellency moved his head from one side to another, and almost unconsciously brought a slice of ham to his mouth, the last one on the plate. But he hardly had time to enjoy it because a subterranean rage filled his mouth with a sharp and dry bitterness which made what he'd just discovered even more unpleasant. Twice now he'd ordered Don Xenaro to have them remove that portion of the journal where the favors received through Saint's intercession were described. And for the second time there it was.

A resident of the city who signed herself "Devout" confessed that her terminal illness had been cured. It had happened after visiting more than eight doctors, passing her pains through the waters of five spas, and taking hundreds of potions and apothecary mixtures without any results. A big lump like an egg in her left breast began to swell one day in a dramatic and alarming way. When it had reached the size of a child's head, there came a suffering like needles inserted into the most sensitive part of her body. Then she remembered Sister Sabina, recited an Ave Maria for the nun's intentions, and the lump disappeared instantly. "Devout" promised to go on her knees from her house to the convent.

A man who concealed his identity behind the word "Repentant" confessed to having received a priceless favor. One Sunday he'd decided with a group of friends to attend an indecent spectacle which he didn't name. He did so with the clear awareness it would offend God, drawn by passion and a perverse curiosity. Back at home that night, he realized with horror that his vision was being taken from him. Within a few minutes he'd gone completely blind, and he heard a booming voice from the sky which condemned his afternoon's behavior. He began to cry inconsolably. Then he remembered the Saint and promised to give four thousand *reales* and a pig to the convent. Some filth, like bird shit, instantly fell from his eyes, and he regained his sight. "Repentant" declared that his promise had already been fulfilled.

Write-ins also came from people who'd found lost objects; from the mother of a family whose son had been going down a bad path and had been saved; from a lady who'd finally managed to free herself from her husband's persistent lust; from a rich thief who'd given back everything he took; from a boy who'd been cured of a malignant intestinal disease; from a priest who'd thrown off a temptation as big as a cow; from a sinner who'd now gone two months without sinning; from a shopkeeper bankrupt and once again rolling in money; from an old widowed man who'd been graced with a visitation...

His Excellency felt dizzy. He left the journal on the table and leaned back against the armchair. A painful fatigue plagued his head. He needed to breathe in some fresh air, maybe forget about the tensions he'd lived with during the summer. The thought of his native city, impossible and far away, alleviated the pain he felt in his forehead for a few seconds. But then the thrashes of his blood beating against his veins came back with more strength. A round and bottomless hole dug deeply into his stomach. He went towards the bathroom at full speed, holding in the urgently rising vomit with his hands.

X

It took him a moment to realize what he was reading, despite the fact that the news came framed on the first page, titled in two columns, and emphasized with wide letters. To him, such a thing was so unthinkable that he had trouble understanding it. Only after several times reciting his own name, which appeared at the end endorsing this alleged "Note from the Episcopacy," did he understand. Then, a bitter and pained groan exited from the depths of his heart, a scream which crashed over and over against the walls of his blood. His eyes searched for the cloudy picture of Christ hanging from the wall. He appeared with his back turned away, indifferent and distant.

He left at a run, took a couple of aimless strolls, opened and closed the door to the bedroom several times, and finally entered the palace's private oratory. A small oil lamp ever so slightly illuminated the baroque darkness of its interior. An old and thick cold accentuated the church's frozen solitude. From high up in the cupola fell a murmur of scared birds that bounced against the stony silence of the walls and roof. Not a single sound came from the morning-time calm within which the building still rested during those hours.

He let himself fall into the recliner, sank his head into his hands, and stayed like that for a long time without doing or thinking anything. A clamor of voices fought inside his brain. He felt distant motions sliding torrentially down the thickness of his veins. An ancient and tribal animosity climbed from the incorruptible and white hardness of his bones to the round and polished opening of his mouth, where it drowned. Ages of rage balled up, vengeful knives rose to find the firmness of his arm, to rehearse the curve of the air.

He spent hours with his back turned to the mystery of forgiveness. The image of a Christ with lash and whip, the accuser in the temple, the scourge of scriveners and hypocritical Pharisees, gave life to a wasp's nest in his chest. None of that turning the other cheek, or calling enemies by the sacred name of brothers, or praying for their conversion to the Lord. Crush them, reduce them to ashes, chase them out, eliminate them... A mixture of feelings of sarcasm, of wounded pride, and of humbled intelligence was shaping his determination.

It took a while for tranquility to return. It came with a creed slowly recited, each one of its words meditated on. Upon finishing, he raised his eyes for the first time, and between the embers of light which flared up in the air he could see the image of Jesus of Nazareth presiding with such a friendly and human expression that it almost made him cry. Calm once again settled inside him, sat nicely on his body, gave him pleasure... The passion defeated, he could now begin to prepare things in the best possible manner.

He exited the church in peace and with the feeling of having defeated someone. Walking towards the office, Saint Paul's comforting words, meditated upon so often, passed through his memory: *Wherefore he that thinketh himself to stand, let him take heed lest he fall. Let no temptation take hold on you, but such as is human. And God is faithful, who will not suffer you to be tempted above that which you are able: but will make also with temptation issue, that you may be able to bear it.* Before opening the door, he got the impression that the mocking smile of a malignant shadow was coming from the darkness.

La Verdad remained on top of the small marble centerpiece, just as he'd left it, beside a small, rose-patterned English plate full of little pieces of cheese. Without sitting down, he read the "Note from the Episcopacy" again, more than anything to convince himself that the state of mind in which he'd left the church still endured. Only a slightly uncomfortable limp reminded him of his trampled dignity. He crossed behind the armchair and went to take his place at the solemn desk. He quickly organized the papers, put *The Imitation of Christ* to one side, and energetically shook the little summoning bell.

As he waited for the attendant, he had a compassionate thought for the Italian from the cinema and his wife. The memory of the child sleeping on the floor at the foot of the piano and the dog sad and tied up awoke an adolescent and sentimental burning in his nostrils. He overcame it by looking out the window and organizing the ideas still floating around in his head. The smiling shadow which had crossed him in the hallway haunted once again from some corner of the room. He looked at the portrait of his predecessor and exchanged a restrained and serious glance with him.

He received the attendant with his hands interlaced, his mouth taut, and his eyes locked. For the first time, Don Xenaro entered that room without a smile on his lips, with his voice drawn back and cautious, and a guilty nervousness which His Excellency didn't bother to ease. He let him remain standing, indifferently observed the anxiety that was etched on the attendant's face, and confidently asked:

"Who is responsible for this disgrace?"

With his eyes turned towards the table near where the bishop pointed with a gesture, and on which *La Verdad* was spread out, Don Xenaro only managed to blurt out:

"I have never counted myself among Your Excellency's enemies."

"I would like it if you answered my question."

"I know nothing about this matter. Maybe it's an error by the newspaper itself. The cinematograph has scandalized quite a few consciences."

The bishop was silent. Don Xenaro's nervousness began to disappear. All that remained visible was the discomfort of remaining on foot, which the attendant made an effort to display with small turns towards one side then the other, as if looking for a place to sit. His Excellency interrupted him:

"Forging a signature is a crime. But above all it's a grave sin. We're Christians."

His allusion to the crime seemed to be more important to the attendant than the reminder about the sin.

"A crime? I still think it must be an error," he said fearfully.

"An error that coincides with the desires of you and others."

"The cinematograph caused a lot of harm. The Saint had revelations."

"You mean Sister Sabina had revelations."

"Sister Sabina is a saint, monsignor."

His Excellency had promised himself not to lose patience with his attendant.

"God and your conscience will know the truth."

Don Xenaro's face lit up with fury. There was in his apparently submissive attitude an internal rage ever more difficult to hide. Only the respect His Excellency inspired in him, along with the weakness conferred upon him by his solitude, managed to keep him within the limits of protocol. Nevertheless, he said:

"Your Excellency seems to be unaware of the hard times facing the Church."

The bishop's silence seemed to give him strength.

"We're being persecuted. Canalejas and Romanones act openly against us. Ever since the barbarian Sagasta rose to power, the campaigns against the clergy are growing. The Krausists have taken over the University. The teaching of religion in school is prohibited. They want to close our academies…"

Don Xenaro was about to cry.

"And what does all this have to do with the matter at hand?" asked His Excellency.

Without lowering the excited tone of his words, deaf to the question just asked of him, the attendant proceeded:

"And meanwhile Your Honor has no qualms with standing against those who are most faithful. It's not a secret to anyone the hostility you feel towards the honorable canon theologian and the contempt with which you treat Sister Sabina."

His Excellency let him speak.

"And Sister Sabina is a saint. The Lord works through her to enlighten us all. By the grace that God deigned to grant her, we are aware of Divine Providence's plans for the diocese. The Lord asks courage and strength of us in this hour of trial. We cannot succumb to the temptation of neglect. His Excellency must make his authority be felt by the enemies of the Church."

"The Church's authority isn't exactly made to be felt with acts like today's," the bishop said, standing up from his chair and allowing his displeasure to come out freely. Then, taking small strides around the office, he continued: "I never thought representatives of Christ would dare to impersonate their prelate."

Don Xenaro persisted:

"Once again I think it must be an error."

"Error or not," His Excellency proceeded, "I demand a public rectification. This very night I'm going to send a clarifying note to the honorable editor of *La Verdad*."

"God writes straight with crooked lines," pronounced the attendant. "The Lord," he continued, "has expressed his anger to Sister Sabina."

His Excellency cut him off:

"Please, don't mix God up in these things."

"Even if the note of condemnation towards the cinematograph is due to an error, this could be the will of the Most High. Sometimes the Lord works in..."

"I'm telling you once again not to mix the Lord up in these miseries," said the bishop, and he drily dismissed his attendant.

XI

He waited three days for the refutation to appear. On the fourth he sent a note to the editor requesting that he stop by the palace. As he waited for him, His Excellency thought about how he knew almost nothing regarding this man whose friends praised his proven loyalty to the Church and his no less well-known faithfulness. Father of fourteen children, he had an intense family life and rarely attended get-togethers and conventions. He consumed his afternoons and a good part of his nights in the editing of the newspaper, where he'd gained renown as a just and proper person, although the majority of his employees accused him of being tight-fisted and miserly. In any case he organized support campaigns for the poor and needy, and gave alms.

His Excellency himself had run into him at a couple of meetings related to the diocese's charitable organization. He remembered him as being silent and gray, introverted and untalkative. On his face he bore the marks of a tormented believer. Nervous blinking and the enraged grimace of brittle hands spoke of long internal battles, possibly of scruples. An experience as drawn out as it was unpleasant of acting as his confessor revealed to the bishop hidden monsters, gigantic ghosts within the soul of that man, the meeting with whom he was starting to worry about.

He wrote the editorials for *La Verdad* and signed his name to a section titled "Christian Battering Ram," sharp and scathing, inflexible and vigorous, written in Castilian, which he devoted to commentating on the current state of national politics. He called Romanones "The Gimp." Of Canalejas he said that his anticlerical fury came from the disaster of his opposition to the University of Madrid's Literature Faculty. He accused him of being "fickle," "a bootlicker," and "an ignorant antediluvian." He predicted a violent death for him, a punishment from God in this current world, a taste of those that were being prepared for him in the next one.

Naturally, he was His Excellency's favorite penman. Simple without being plain, clear and precise, without any more adornments than were strictly necessary, he possessed a pleasant fluidity, beneath which could be discerned a disciplined effort at pruning which his enemies, especially the modernist boys from the journal *El pájaro verde*, exaggerators and smokers of hashish, theosophical and feathered, didn't give due credit. However His Excellency had grown accustomed to reading beyond the hostile inflexibility of his thought and above the irrational phobias he displayed.

At this stage, the bishop was ignorant as to why *La Verdad* hadn't published the note he sent. He knew of the relationship between the editor and the theologian, an assiduous collaborator on the newspaper, but he trusted the former's healthy conscience, based on the ever clearer picture he was forming of him. For an instant he wondered whether he might not be creating an ideal in line with the needs he felt, but he didn't take long to convince himself of the objectivity of his assessments. And he kept waiting.

Even though they hadn't set a time for the meeting, he assumed that the editor wouldn't be late. He opted to wait for him by strolling around the office, but when he realized those down below would be listening happily to his nervous pacing about, he opted to occupy one of the stone benches in the bay of the window. The first rains had arrived a while ago, and through the panes, from between the palm trees in the entryway, he could make out a melancholy yellow of fallen leaves. Over the stones of the street came the clop of the twelve-o'clock coach, with the last spare horses asking for feed and the numb and wet coachman on top of the driver's seat. Summer remained far away.

Rain always produced an intimate and quiet nostalgia in him, which he fought against without much conviction. He remembered his native Mondoñedo, the happiness of the Remedios Shrine, the murmur of the Old Fountain, the Pasatempo Bridge, the colors and the shouts of puppet-show nights in the Cantón. It distressed him to know himself and to feel himself exiled, far away from his own. For the first two years he'd still spent the summer in his ancestral home on Templarios Street, with his beautiful and old little mother, surrounded by the respect and affection of various canons and seminary professors, good Latinists, excellent theologians, people of good conversation and good appetite, in the company of whom His Excellency had lived unforgettable days.

With the emotion still wet in his eyes, he heard a soft knock on the door. He ran to open. Moved by the friendly impulse of the thoughts this visit had just cut off, he raised his arms for an embrace, but encountered a stinginess which reminded him that the image of the editor he'd been elaborating during his wait wasn't false. This calmed him.

"Your Excellency will pardon my delay," the director said at the same time as he got straight down onto a knee to kiss the prelate's ring.

"Not a problem," responded the latter as he helped him get up.

Both of them remained standing for a moment.

"What happened is that Don Telesforo held me up," the journalist apologized. Then he added:

"He'd like us to give him an entire page for the problem of education on Sunday. He's worried."

His Excellency gained even more confidence. The reference to Don Telesforo, purely informative and lacking any kind of emotional connotation, seemed to him the best proof of his interlocutor's neutrality and good faith. He invited him to sit, calmly placed his hands on his hips, and began to speak:

"I assume you must know the reason for this call."

"It isn't difficult for me to imagine," the editor responded.

The bishop paused, rocked his body back and forth, and added:

"The condemnatory note about the cinematograph isn't of my authorship."

"I found that out when I read the rectifying document Your Honor sent. It was a surprise to me."

There wasn't a single hint in his words which allowed for an interpretation of the thoughts going through his head. His Excellency looked to break the sterile equilibrium of the conversation, but was unable to. With this intention he said:

"A disgrace! A true disgrace!"

The editor listened to him in silence.

"You must understand," proceeded the bishop, "that this confusion has to be cleared up."

His Excellency's words were lost in the air once again.

"What's more," he went on, "there are third parties in this matter who could be seriously wronged."

"Is Your Honor referring to the Italian?" the editor finally asked.

"To the Italian and his family."

"A pirate, monsignor. A real bandit. As far as the family is concerned, that man and that woman have a common-law marriage."

His Excellency adopted an expectant attitude. His interlocutor made a motion that he would continue to speak:

"I don't think Your Excellency needs to worry. Ever since they came to the city, they haven't been known to set foot in church on a single Sunday. Bad people, monsignor. You can be sure."

There was something in the man's firmness when speaking about his fellow humans that irritated His Excellency. He opted to return to the original topic:

"I would like for the note I sent you to go out as soon as possible."

For the first time since he'd arrived, the editor hinted at a gaunt and ascetic smile:

"I see Your Honor is obsessed with this issue. If you'll permit me, I would say it is all unimportant."

"Did you say it was unimportant?"

There was a tone of concern in His Excellency's question.

"Yes," responded the editor. "What's more," he continued, "I should tell you that based on the information I have, the note was very well received in the city. Not even the liberal parts protested. There's no one who would pay a penny for that cinematograph contraption."

His Excellency looked within himself, delving into the open wound in search of a reason to rise up to those words, but an unconquerable and distant fatigue sank him into a walled silence. The editor's words flew around in front of his eyes like monstrous, headless birds.

XII

He felt a swollen heat lighting up his face. His forehead started to hurt in the place where his hand had supported all the weight of a tense worry that had already lasted a couple of hours. A gritty discomfort forced him to keep his eyes half open. The darkness outside was absolute. The rain scratched against the windowpanes and a crazy and uncontrollable wind went about putting fear in the streets. Every once in a while a lightning bolt opened up the sky for a few seconds, and what remained in the air afterwards was a bluish anticipation which erupted in a downpour against the mountains. It was cold.

His Excellency had spent the whole day in his office. He'd cancelled audiences since the day before and had requested that he not be bothered. He'd substituted lunch for a *café con leite* and a couple of bananas and had easily gotten by without the short *sesta* in the Saint Ignatius Lounge. Although he hadn't done it intentionally, that was actually his monthly retreat. The bishop lacked only the company of the vicar, charged in times past with making a bit of conversation, and of course he missed him.

Before his eyes he currently held the paper with the notes he'd been taking throughout the morning. Beneath the epigraph, "Matter: Note of Rectification," he'd written: "*Things odious to God. Six things there are, which the Lord hateth, and the seventh his soul detesteth: Haughty eyes, a lying tongue, hands that shed innocent blood, A heart that deviseth wicked plots, feet that are swift to run into mischief, A deceitful witness that uttereth lies, and him that soweth discord among brethren* (Proverbs 6:16-19)." These words were inscribed in a firm and clear hand, with the calm of someone who looks to support their thoughts through the tranquility of writing.

He read the Biblical words again and once more experienced the comforting feeling of a spiritual energy which was taking over his soul little by little. Then he realized that the congestion was disappearing from his face and a freshness seemingly blown in from outside was alleviating the pain he felt in his temples. It had stopped raining and some voices could be heard in the street. The drunks, the last taverns nearby on Danger Alley being closed, complained unconvincingly about authority as they left fumbling their way through the darkness towards home.

His Excellency grabbed another sheet of untrimmed paper, dipped his pen in the writing desk's silver inkwell, and without a moment of pause, as if he had it well thought out, started to write the note of rectification for *El Liberal*. He searched for simple words, avoided the stereotypical formulas of priestly language, contained himself within the ascetic limits of a voluntarily simple syntax, and in fourteen lines, not a single word more, recorded what he wanted to say. He read it calmly afterwards, jotted down a couple of possible changes in pencil, and began to write the whole text again. The second version seemed better to him.

It had been three days since, going up to San Martiño on his way to the almshouse, upon turning the corner onto Arcediagos Street, His Excellency had run into a group of people having a get-together right in the middle of the road. When they saw him, they all turned around to greet him with their top hats, accompanying the gesture with a distinguished and marked reverence. The bishop returned their greeting with a motion of his hand which sought to be affectionate and courteous. One of them was the editor of *El Liberal*.

His Excellency had heard more than enough opinions about this man. His enemies, who seemed to be many, accused him of being a twenty-seventh-degree mason, asserted that he was a disciple of the German philosopher Krause, and denounced him as being obstinately and furiously anticlerical. His press campaigns, insistent and merciless, had embittered the last years of the prelate's virtuous predecessor. His friends, on the other hand, praised his sense of friendship, the integrity of his conduct, and the elegance and attentiveness of his behavior. He was a good penman, although a bit too rhetorical for the bishop's taste, but that didn't stop him from reading his paper every day.

Surrounding the newspaper he edited was gathered a small group of the city's intellectual minds. The money came from the congressman Anselmo Pérez, a brilliant and theatrical man, who'd survived over fifteen duels, seven of them with pistols. He maintained that baptism was evidence of barbarity, a useless torture which was dangerous for the health of little children, and that only those adults who voluntarily desired it should be baptized. Of communion he said it was the last lingering remnant of cannibalism in civilized Europe, and suggested that those who practiced it should receive the consideration and treatment of primitive and savage men. He was a thorn in the side of the theologian, who he privately called "Beautiful Lola." He stirred up a lot of commotion in Madrid and for years had maintained an unending litigation with the clergy due to the cathedral's bells, the chiming of which he sought to restrict.

His confidant in the city was Don Luís Limia, a lawyer known by the awful name of "Pussylips." He was in the group His Excellency had surprised in the street. An incorrigible bachelor, he'd won deserved renown as a womanizer. He had familiarities with ten lady friends, most of them from the country. Some people allotted him eighteen bastard children, all made during the hunting season, when the lawyer would close his office for a couple of weeks and disappear surrounded by dogs, rifle on his back, in search of rabbit holes among the woodlands and whins of the mountains. He had come to blows with the honorable abbot of Vilaseca da Raia, at one time his good friend and hunting partner, seemingly due to a loose woman who they split fifty-fifty, and about whom they'd ended up having a disagreement. Even though he wasn't and didn't try to be a man of letters, Limia's influence on the newspaper was reputed to be quite large.

The executor of his will within the paper was the writer Vázquez, a former seminarian who'd left with a reputation of intelligence among his companions. Socially marginalized by his reserved personality and by a forced marriage, he worked as a man in the shadows. Not a single line was published in the newspaper without first receiving his seal of approval. Little was known about his ideas, but his defector's radical anticlericalism was public. He had twice gotten into a fist fight with the editor of *La Verdad*, who he always referred to as "The Honorary Priest," and had taken aim at Sister Sabina. He'd called her "hysterical," "frustrated cow," "charlatan," and "viper." He'd won a lawsuit against the theologian for libel. He'd baptized him with the name "Scorpion."

These men's biographies were going through His Excellency's head one by one. In truth he wasn't afraid of any of them, and couldn't even avoid looking at some of them with a certain sympathy. In any case he experienced a feeling he was unable to identify. He wasn't sure if it was doubt or fear. But an annoying discomfort beat within his chest and accelerated the in-and-of-itself slow rhythm of a heart that was beginning to display the first signs of fatigue. He remembered his father discreetly feeling his own pulse at lunchtime, after an entire morning of work in the office dealing with sufferings and calamities. His Excellency didn't feel strong.

The apocryphal note in *La Verdad* had wounded him. He had just learned how there are incidents in a man's life capable of marking him forever, of definitively altering his life. It was neither news nor a surprise, but it disgusted him that such occurrences should be so little controllable, should depend so little on the will of those who suffered them. Maybe this was a clear manifestation of Divine Providence's hidden and mysterious plans. He remembered the Book of Job and a cascade of immense words, big like boulders, passed through his memory and flooded down to his lips. He prayed with them.

The day after tomorrow, perhaps the very next day, *El Liberal* would publish the refutation on its front page: "The Bishop of the Diocese Did Not Condemn the Cinematograph." He could easily imagine the question which the writer Vázquez would add beneath the black letters of the headline: "So who is responsible for the note published days ago by *La Verdad*?" And the expected insinuation: "Sinister forces embedded in the bishop's palace itself could be subjecting the honorable bishop to an overwhelming siege with the shameful intention of aligning him with superstition, intolerance, fanaticism, and insanity." The climax wasn't hard to predict either: "Will the persecutors of Galileo and John of Nepomuk, of Hus and Calvin, be able to triumph in their intentions?"

The sure anticipation of the future brought a savor of triumph to His Excellency's spirits, maybe an exciting taste of revenge. He preferred to think about it as a case of justice restored. When he let his tired body fall into bed at the end of the day, along with sleep and just as punctual, came the forgotten pleasure of a cozy and warm tranquility.

XIII

The reaction from *La Verdad*, prompt and forceful, didn't take His Excellency by surprise. The conservative newspaper accused its rival of inventing the information and manipulating reality, with the goal of bringing sympathy to Mr. Canalejas' anticlerical cause. That the diocesan clergy caught in the middle would be put into an undervalued position, with insinuations as wild as they were vile, and that the venerable figure of an exemplary prelate would be questioned, little could it matter to a newspaper which had declared its purpose, easily verifiable for any reader, of contributing to the smear campaign unleashed against the Catholic Church.

His Excellency experienced a slight sentimental reaction when he read the adjective "exemplary" applied to his person, but he didn't take long to regain his peace of mind and put himself in a position as far as possible from those incidents that so directly affected him. He felt calm. More than hear, down below he could discern a murmur of comments and criticisms, of voices and threats. The name of the congressman Anselmo Pérez was neatly uttered on two occasions, and someone shoutingly referred to the writer Vázquez.

At midday Don Xenaro came up to communicate to him that, during mass, Sister Sabina had suffered a faint followed by vomits of blood, and the doctors seemed pessimistic regarding her health. The news had run quickly through the city and people were nervous. No one doubted that the cause of the sister's sudden indisposition was the antireligious campaign initiated once again by *El Liberal*, motivated by the "Note from the Episcopacy" about the cinematograph. Such was the atmosphere being breathed among the upper neighborhoods that he himself had needed to convince a group of boys who were threatening to attack the newspaper that they should return to their houses. In such a situation, His Excellency couldn't remain quiet. Some words from him were needed in order to provide guidance and advice.

"Your Honor should refute that news statement," he said with his voice shaky and a look of pleading in his eyes.

"There's nothing to refute. That news statement says the truth," the bishop responded, without letting himself be influenced by the emotion which had overwhelmed the priest.

A shadow of concern and surprise crossed the latter's face.

"You mean that that note was sent by Your Excellency?"

"Exactly," the prelate punctuated.

Forgetting all about protocol in his hurry, the attendant exited the episcopal office at a run. Before closing the door, as if to correct what must not have seemed to him a very respectful action, he tried a bow which was meant to be solemn, but which was nothing more than ridiculous.

His Excellency returned calmly to his desk. The voices continued down below. With his mind on the words he'd just heard, concerned about the nun's health and its consequences, he routinely dealt with a couple of protocols, answered some pending letters, and recited the Angelus. Upon finishing, he left for the dining room. Seated in the leather chair, at the head of that great rectangular table adorned with bronze candelabras and covered with the ever so pure linen tablecloth, he felt alone. While serving him the soup, with the beginnings of tears in his eyes and emotion hanging off his lips, the servant concernedly asked:

"Does Your Honor think the Saint will be saved?"

"The Lord's will shall be done," answered His Excellency with a hint of routine in his voice.

The helper finished pouring the soup onto the plate. Then he moved away in silence, but before reaching the door he paused to say:

"They say it's the liberals' fault, that they put a blasphemy in the newspaper. There's so much nastiness in this world, sir."

His Excellency remained silent. He ate the soup without desire. In front of a baked red sea bream, splendidly garnished and nicely plated, he made an effort, but he wasn't able to get through two bites. He left the dessert untouched. With his body half shrunken by the cold and the damp, he stood up without responding and left for the Saint Ignatius Lounge. The flame in the fireplace received him with loving warmth. First he heated up both sides of his hands, next he put out his shoes with their soles facing towards the flames, and finally he went to sit in the armchair.

Despite being foggy, the window allowed the tired light of an energyless sun to pass through. It had rained endlessly throughout the whole morning. Upon crashing against the windows, the water burst into little stars. It might already be snowing in the mountains. The coziness of the fire seeping into His Excellency's muscles forecast the long winter. With it came old melancholies and a morbid happiness, simultaneously accepted and rejected, that dug him in for hours and hours, silent and sleepy, in front of the fireplace with a book in his hand. Worried by Don Xenaro's words, he couldn't fully enjoy the moment. He opened a copy of *Treasure Island*, by Robert Louis Stevenson, but was unable to read a single page.

The many bitternesses provided to him by the governance of the diocese now came to his head all at once. The flame rose deeply and powerfully, evocatively and nostalgically before his absent eyes, off sifting through his memories. He'd dreamt of being a bishop ever since he was a boy. Full of emotion, he remembered the afternoon on which his mother and aunts, over and over again with the needle on the garden balcony, between stories, had sewn him a chasuble and an alb so that he could play pretend priest. He gave mass on top of a box covered by a sheet sprinkled with carnations. The chalice was a glass for eating strawberries, and the host, a real host they'd given him with the cut-outs in the parish. The whole family attended. Aunt Dora always ended up laughing out loud. Then he stepped down from the platform he used as a presbytery, got up onto a bench, and uttered a terrible sermon against women. At the end they all had a picnic together and his father told stories about Frouseira Castle and the *Mariscal* Pedro Pardo de Cela, about Pasatempo Bridge and the justice of Kings.

He'd already entered the seminary saying he wanted to be a bishop with a horse. From the beginning he'd been a good student. He finished his degree quickly and brilliantly. Then came the years as prefect of philosophers and afterwards the assignment as teacher of morals. Joyful years. Friends got together at night for *tertulias*, hours and hours of enjoying the incomparable pleasure of chit-chat, of exchanging ideas and opinions without any other worry besides spending a pleasant evening and taking a break from work in the classrooms and in the isolated and fertile silence of the dormitories. The rumor of his episcopal nomination had reached him during one of those *tertulias*. Remembering the excitement and the concerns of those days, looking back on the long story of his stay at the head of the diocese, His Excellency fell asleep.

An agitated ringing of the church bells woke him up. They were warning of a fire from San Francisco Church. He got up immediately and went to look out the window. He didn't see anything. He went towards the office. From there he was able to observe a dense *fumata* which rose imposingly from the Vilachá neighborhood outside the city. The Barbagelatta cinema was burning. Enormous flames were leaping above the shacks. A gesticulating and nervous crowd shifted back and forth, running from one side to another with pots of water and brooms in their hands. The ashen smell reached as far as the palace. His Excellency moved away. He took a seat, rested his head in his hands, and stayed like that for a good bit of time. Then he recited an Our Father for the Italians.

That same afternoon, little before the rosary, he found out about another disgrace. A small group of cloaked figures had attacked the home of the writer Vázquez. They tied him and his wife to the kitchen table and then beat them and left them for dead, with their blood running along the floor and both of them unconscious. The alarm was sounded by their six-year-old child, who'd witnessed the scene in terror through the spyglass of a door. The doctor was with them now, trying to mend the carnage caused by others.

Powerless before such evil, His Excellency suffered an attack of desperation. Still dominated by rage and pain, he took a sheet of paper, gripped his pen, and began to write: "When Christ no longer works to save, but rather to burn, to hit, to scandalize, one must have the courage to reject Christ, to spit in his face, to bury him in hell. If the peaceful Christ of forgiveness no longer works for us during our moments of madness, let us curse him, let us condemn him as a heretic, for falsifying here on earth the cruel image of the God of the Old Testament, for not fulfilling his duty to smite our enemies with lightning and burn them with fire."

He dipped his pen in the inkwell once more and continued: "When people of habit and cassock abandon their sacred mission as shepherds and become thugs and arsonists, whether directly or through other people, they too become unworthy and make possible the persecution of the Church which they represent. It could not then be said that the persecutors are simply evil. In fact it would have to be concluded that they are the agents through which the Lord works to purify the Church he established."

Upon finishing, he reread what he'd written, signed below with the pseudonym "Aletheios," and put it into a white folder addressed to *El Liberal*. Then he went into the oratory to pray.

XIV

Five more articles by "Aletheios" followed that one, all written in the same critical tone, with the same Biblical indignation with which he had written the first: the idea of a sectarian and hate-sowing Church produced anguish and disgust in him. A thick and silent violence covered the city like a giant thundercloud. The congressman Anselmo Pérez had met with the Civil Guard and requested protection for the newspaper, for the writers and their families. Barbagelatta and his own had had to run away with only the clothes on their backs, followed closely by a screaming mob, who three squadrons of soldiers had had difficulty containing.

The reactions against the articles didn't take long to arrive. The harshest was presented in Castilian on the Third Sunday of Advent, during the religious services held in the cathedral. From the pulpit Don Telesforo vehemently attacked "that coward who hides behind such a noble name." He called him "perverse spirit," "enemy of God," and "Satan's penman." He spoke about persecution, predicted hard times for the Church, and appealed for an energetic defense. He said it was true that the first Christians had allowed themselves to be killed *quia vires non habebant*, "because they had no strength," but it was not going to happen again because it had to be demonstrated to the persecutors that all of Christ's power is with his children and only them will he aid.

An allusion to "those who drink their philosophical poison in foreign books" made His Excellency think the canon identified "Aletheios" as the editor of *El Liberal*. Rather than amusing him, this lack of insight produced a certain unease. But he was unsettled even more by the final words when, serenely, without even raising his voice, in a merely informative tone he announced a campaign for the coming days which certain devout people were going to sponsor with the goal of correcting such evil, so they could stop in time the harmful effects of the venom which had so freely and without any kind of institutional reaction been spilled onto people's souls. It would begin that same afternoon with a procession of penance.

The ambiguity of the language employed by the theologian concealed worrying threats which he didn't fail to notice: His Excellency knew very well where that crusading spirit might originate from. For this reason, when he was undressing in the sacristy, with the alb still covering his head, and he heard the dry and formal *Prosit* from Don Telesforo, he hurried to prevent the latter from being able to leave without first hearing some words. While the canon removed his surplice, he said:

"I trust your good sense will know how to avoid irreparable harms."

The theologian stared at him fixedly, without any emotion in his gaze.

"The faithful demand an episcopal condemnation of the author of these indecent articles. They believe His Excellency's weaknesses and complacencies before the Church's enemies have already brought much harm."

The bishop, slightly unsettled, waited a moment before responding. Then he said:

"The Church's mission is not to condemn."

"In the field of doctrine," responded the theologian with a sarcastic smile, "Your Excellency's word is not exactly characterized by its brilliance."

The insolence of the provocation failed to disrupt the prelate's peaceful nature, as he left for the inside of the cathedral without a response. Upon passing in front of the Saint Euphemia Chapel, in the ambulatory, he felt his legs folding out from under him all of a sudden. He pushed himself up against the metal grating and tried to keep himself standing, grabbing forcefully onto the iron bars. His heart was drumming agitated and tired within his ribcage, and an unpleasant taste of sulfur numbed his tongue. His consciousness was swept from him for a moment and he thought he was going to fall, but his arms, nearly embedded into the metalwork, prevented him from ending up on the floor.

Objects, blurred and hazy for a few instants, took a while to regain their complete clarity. With his legs limp and a cold stinging that spread down his body, His Excellency continued along his path wobbly and unsteady. Going up the stairs took some effort.

He reached the second floor sweating and breathless. He entered the bedroom and threw his clothes onto the bed. With his eyes closed, protecting himself from a painful brightness, he spent a couple of hours resting to see if he could regain the strength he lacked. He tried to get up twice, but both times he had to return to the same position as before. A nausea that rose from the upper part of his stomach to his neck forced him to remain lying down against his will. Shortly before the lunch hour, Don Xenaro came to worry over him. His Excellency requested that he leave him be, that he felt perfectly fine, that he just wanted to rest.

The afternoon, now somewhat recovered, he spent in the Saint Ignatius Lounge, with a blanket over his legs, immobile and alone, in front of the fireplace. The flame revived his blood, and that icy murmur which had echoed obsessively within his bones since morning left his body. Cheerful, he picked up the Stevenson novel and, bit by bit, occasionally going back over what he'd already read, he managed to get through a few pages. He was interrupted by a clamor of prayers and songs rising from the street. He peeked out the window and saw a procession in double file, men and women marching in bare feet and with lit candles in their hands. Sister Sabina went in front, faint and held up in the arms of two nuns. At her side, face white and jaw muscles tense, hands straight and head devoutly bent, was the theologian. He walked rigid and serious, upright and bright, with his eyes on the ground. Behind, Don Xenaro and some other cassocks. Next up, boys and girls from the city schools and a flood of people singing songs of penance and forgiveness. It seemed to His Excellency like an image of another time, of a faraway era.

The twangy and nasal music of the Castilian *Perdón, oh Dios mío* drilled into his ears and wrapped him in a gooey sadness like a snake around his heart. From the balconies in front, men and women on their knees, hands fervently gathered into their chests, prayed as the retinue passed. A soldier walked with a kind of banner, on the blue cloth of which could be read: "The enemies of the Saint are the enemies of God." He was followed by a group of old people from the nursing home, numb and quiet, with images of Sister Sabina in their hands. A one-legged man with crutches walked in hops, conducting his recitation of the rosary from the back, reciting his Ave Marias at a shout.

They passed slowly in front of the palace, many of them turning their curious eyes towards the main balcony. It was then that His Excellency felt his legs fold out from under him again. He grabbed onto the curtains in order not to fall and held on like that for a couple of minutes, until he was able to get to the armchair. A stabbing pain like a sharp knife went through his chest from one side to the other. He called out for help several times, but his voice bounced against the walls of the room, went echoing down through the stairs, and was lost among the singing in the street. Suddenly the world began to be just noise, an enormous seashell putting his brain to sleep.

When he came to, he was soaked. He felt a pleasant drowsiness caressing his body and a desire to stay there forever, lying softly down on the floor, uneager to stand up and go on living. If death was similar to what had just happened, he wouldn't mind dying very much. He almost felt upset at having regained consciousness, content as he was. Even so he got up. Supporting himself on the walls, he was able to reach the office.

He looked at himself in the cornucopia mirror that adorned the outer wall: his eyes sunken into a saggy mass of brown skin, his white and pointed nose, his copper cheeks, his pale forehead. He stared at his wrists. They seemed transparent. The blue of his veins went up without any strength to lose itself in the flabby thickness of his arm. With his palms turned upwards, slightly bent over, as if he lacked the strength to support the weight of his head, His Excellency saw himself as the tragic representation of an animal forced to stand on its hind legs. From a distance, possibly from the cathedral area, came shouts uttered in unison. They had the rhythm of an obsessive and threatening harmony, the melodic curve of a war chant. Amazed by his own image and frightened by the voices he heard, the bishop went to sit down.

On top of the table, a copy of the Gospels, which he kissed softly and then brought lovingly to his chest. To his left, the small baroque *Pietà* carved out of jet, a gift from his colleagues for the twenty-fifth anniversary of his priesthood. To his right, a little lacquer box. He opened it. He took out the rosary that had been his mother's and held it in his closed hand for a few instants, squeezing the cross and the beads until he felt pain.

Opposite him, the writing desk, and to one side, a tiny mountain of sheets of untrimmed paper. He took one, spread it out in front, on top of the violet leather handbook, and dipped his pen in the inkwell.

With angled and shaky handwriting, restfully, he began to write: "We, the doctor Fernando Fanego, bishop of this diocese by the Grace of God and the Holy Apostolic See, make known to all its members: That a series of articles having been published in one of this city's newspapers which may contribute to the disturbance of the necessary peace of mind, and desiring above all human consideration the spiritual well-being of our dear Church, we expressly condemn the aforementioned articles and we command its author, whosoever that person who hides behind the pseudonym 'Aletheios' may be, in the interest of everyone's well-being, especially the community which has been entrusted to us by the Lord, to alter their course so that the peace we all desire can be attained."

Upon reaching this point, two round and fat tears fell onto the center of the paper, over the name "Aletheios," which instantly became a hazy and blue puddle. The cathedral bells began to chime the funeral toll, the mournful lament for a soul on the verge of giving an account. His Excellency tore up the smudged sheet, grabbed another, and making a huge effort to move his arm, he started to write again.

Rodeira (Cangas), 1979

Jacob Rogers
is a translator based in Asheville, North Carolina. He holds degrees
in Literature and Spanish from the University of North Carolina
at Asheville and translates primarily Galician fiction and poetry.
He has published translations of an excerpt of Xabier López López's
award-winning novel *Chains*, as well as selected fiction and poetry
by Begoña Paz from her story collection *The Wound* and her
poetry collection *The Bad Life*. Forthcoming projects include
work by Xavier Queipo, Xurxo Borrazás, and more by Begoña Paz.
His Excellency is his first book-length publication.

GALICIAN

CLASSICS

www.ingramcontent.com/pod-product-compliance
Lightning Source LLC
Chambersburg PA
CBHW030528260626
47157CB00005B/1931